MW01054157

Century Farm

Century Farm

One Hundred Years on a Family Farm

by Cris Peterson
with photographs by Alvis Upitis

BOYDS MILLS PRESS

9-99

Text copyright © 1999 by Cris Peterson

Photographs copyright © 1999 by Alvis Upitis, except those appearing
on pages 1, 5, 6, 10, 12, 13, 14, 16, 17, 18, 20, 24, and 29,
which are taken from the Peterson family album.

Published by Caroline House

Boyds Mills Press, Inc.

A Highlights Company

815 Church Street

Honesdale, Pennsylvania 18431

Printed in China

Publisher Cataloging-in-Publication Data

Peterson, Cris

Century farm / by Cris Peterson.—1st ed.

[32]p. : col. ill. ; cm.

Summary: The story of a 100-year-old family farm in Wisconsin
is told in photographs and in anecdotes about the three generations
of Petersons who have owned and farmed the land.

ISBN 1-56397-710-9

1. Farm life—Wisconsin—Juvenile literature [1. Farm life—Wisconsin.]
I. Title.

636.2/ 142 [E]—dc21   1999   AC   CIP

Library of Congress Catalog Card Number 98-71792

First edition, 1999

The text of this book is set in 16–point Esprit book.

10 9 8 7 6 5 4 3 2 1

To Ben, Matt, and Caroline
—C.P.

To the Petersons,
for ten years of friendship
—A.U.

*Here's what our farmhouse looked like in 1910,
when my great-grandparents and their family
and friends proudly showed off their new cars.*

I know a farm that's almost as old as dirt. It's a century farm—one hundred years old.

The barn is old. The house is old. The granary is old.

The people who built the farm have died. The first cows and chickens and sheep are all gone.

One hundred years is a long time....

But this old farm is still alive. Young cows graze in the pasture. Young crops in the fields reach for the sun. Young kittens totter around on hay bales in the hayloft. And young kids still care for their cattle in the old barn.

When they were younger, my kids liked to play with our dogs and cats in the hayloft. The animals loved it, but the kids weren't much help with chores!

*Here I am in our old barn milking
Bonnie, one of our best cows.*

I know because I own this farm. I grew up in the
middle of the century in the middle of America on this
middle-sized, Midwestern farm.

When I rode my bike up and down the barn walk
while Mom and Dad worked, I didn't know my great-
grandfather had built the barn from trees cut right here
on the land. When I learned to milk the cows, I seldom
stopped to think that my grandmother had milked cows
by hand in the same stall.

When I first drove a tractor in the fields, it didn't occur to me that I was plowing the same soil Grandpa had plowed with horses. But when I finally purchased the farm from Grandpa, I was continuing a tradition that began way back before the turn of the century.

When Grandpa plowed with horses, he could do an acre a day. With this four-bottom plow, we can cover twenty-five acres in a day.

Way back then, my great-grandfather moved to northern Wisconsin from Sweden. When he married my great-grandmother in 1893, she was a widow with ten children living in a log house on this land. She had a few cows, a few chickens, and a small flock of sheep.

My great-grandmother's children were almost grown-up when my great-grandfather joined the family.

My great-grandfather bought a sawmill that same year. He cut trees from our land and sawed lumber for a house, a barn, and a granary. By 1896, he had all new buildings and a new son—my grandfather. By the time Grandpa was old enough to help with the farm work, there were a dozen cows grazing in the pasture and ample crops growing in the cleared fields.

Every spring, Grandpa plowed the soil and seeded
oats, rye, and barley. Then he planted corn. When the
rains fell and the sun baked the earth, he said you could
almost hear that corn grow.

Each planting season still starts when I plant alfalfa
and corn in that same old dirt. The corn still reaches for
the sun and whispers in the wind.

When summer days were the hottest and driest, Grandpa forked hay onto flat, creaky wagons drawn by horses. He used grapple hooks to lift dusty heaps of hay into the hayloft where it was spread in knee-deep layers.

I'll bet some of that old hay is still in our hayloft at the very bottom. But now I chop our hay and pack it into bunker silos. Then we load it into a mixer wagon, mix it up with corn and other grains, and feed it to our cows.

Haying back in Grandpa's time was a slow, hot job. It took hours of work with a pitchfork to make a load like this.

Great-Grandma, Dad, and Grandma, are standing in front of a steam thresher that traveled from farm to farm with a crew of six men. Dad remembers the steam whistle blowing as the engine came down the road at four o'clock in the morning. It woke the whole neighborhood.

In late summer, Grandpa harvested the grain with a horse-drawn binder. He piled the sheaves into prickly, cone-shaped stacks. Then a clanking, dust-spewing steam thresher separated the grain from the chaff.

Today I harvest grain from the same fields with a machine called a combine. The combine cuts and threshes the grain before pouring it into a huge hopper.

Grandpa stands by a shock of corn that's nearly ten feet tall.

After the first frost, Grandpa cut the corn by hand and stacked it in tall shocks. It took ten men and ten teams of horses to haul that corn to the silo and chop it for winter cattle feed.

Today my wife and I still harvest the corn after the first frost. But we chop it with a forage chopper pulled behind a tractor. Our equipment allows us to do the work of those ten men and their teams of horses.

My wife, Cris, usually drives the tractor when we chop corn silage.

Grandma cooked meals for all those workers on a wood stove in the farm kitchen. She also heated water for washing clothes, a job done outside most of the year. It took a small mountain of firewood to keep the house warm in winter and the stove going all year long.

Today, we cook our family's meals in that same kitchen. But when we make cookies, we use an electric mixer and an electric oven.

Every summer Grandma had a big garden. She grew tomatoes, potatoes, onions, and beans. Cucumbers climbed up fences, and peas climbed up poles. Flowers grew everywhere—hollyhocks, phlox, iris, and roses. She canned bushels of sweet corn, tomatoes, and beans. Hundreds of jars of home-grown fruits and vegetables stood in neat rows in her root cellar.

Hollyhocks sometimes grow eight feet tall by our house. The plants are descended from the original ones Grandma grew.

Our family still plants tomatoes and potatoes in the
same garden soil Grandma did. And we grow phlox and
morning glories by the porch door.

Grandma was good with the cows, and they gave lots of milk for her.

Along with housework and gardening, Grandma milked a dozen cows by hand both morning and evening. As our farm began to specialize more and more in dairy production, Grandma used milking machines to milk twenty cows.

When my parents married, they helped Grandma and Grandpa with the chores. Dad also had a job off the farm. He and my mother lived next to the big farmhouse in the summer kitchen.

Years later when I took over the farm, Mom helped me milk thirty cows a day. Then, after I got married, my wife and I milked forty cows while our kids rode their bikes up and down the barn walk.

My wife, Cris, spends a good part of every day working with the cows.

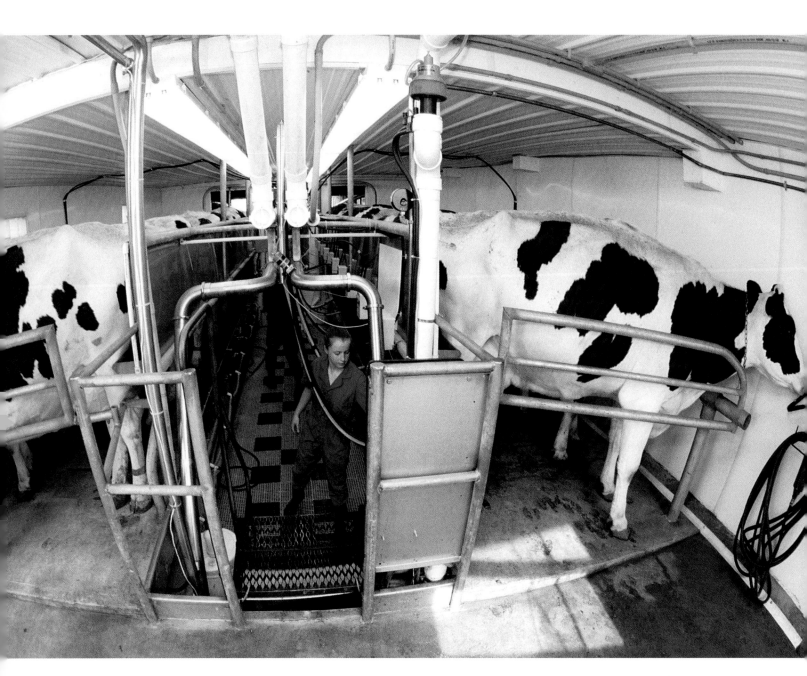

In our new milking parlor my daughter, Caroline, can milk twice as many cows as we used to in the same amount of time.

*My dad and I look over the plans for our new barn.
We're excited to see this big, new building take shape.*

Today with our children and our employees we
milk two hundred cows in a milking parlor we built
inside that same old barn surrounded by the same fields.
The cows will soon live in a breezy free stall barn that is
being built in the old pasture behind the barn. Dad drives
out from town every day to help with all the extra work
as we expand our dairy.

*My sons, Matt and Ben, give their dog
Dundee a workout chasing golf balls.*

But work isn't all we've ever done here. Back at the turn of the century, sheep nibbled the grass in the field south of our house until it was so short that my great-uncle could practice golfing there. Tree stumps and sheep sometimes got in the way.

Today we golf in town, but each spring my sons still practice driving golf balls across that same field.

On gray winter days, my great-grandfather used hand tools and pine lumber to build rowboats from patterns he had brought from Sweden. In the summer, Sundays were spent fishing for bass from one of those boats on a nearby lake.

Today my kids paddle a canoe on that same lake when they fish for bass.

Great-grandpa B.J. rides in the bow of his homemade boat.

So much has changed in one hundred years, but many things have stayed the same. We still work together when a cow needs help giving birth to a calf. We still grow hollyhocks in the same garden where Grandma grew them decades ago. And we still plant in the same soil that grew the timber for our house and barn and granary.

As the kids were growing up we often worked together when a new calf was born.

*My family gathered recently for this picture on a
summer afternoon before the boys returned to college.*

My kids have grown up on this farm, just as I did,
and my father and grandfather before me. They still play
in the hay. They're learning to drive tractors and care for
the cattle. And they're learning to love the land like I do.

Generations of my family have come and gone, each one adding to and changing the farm. Someday my children and grandchildren may work the same land that I have. With each new planting season, with each new generation, this century farm is reborn.